Contents

Chapter 1
Me and Mia

It is 3.35pm.

In the last five minutes, *this* happened:

1. The school bell rang.

2. My friend Mia yelled, “Run!”

3. We ran out of class.

4. Our teacher Miss West yelled, “Don’t run!”

5. We ignored her.

6. The number 39 bus pulled up by the school gate.

7. Mia grabbed my arm and we jumped on first.

8. All the people who had been waiting in line grumbled and tutted at us.

9. I felt bad but Mia just grinned and shouted, “Sorry! It’s an emergency!” at them all.

Mia cracks me up.

She is *so* funny.

And cheeky.

It’s now 3.36pm and we flop down on the very back seat of the top deck of the bus.

We always sit up here. We love to look out the window and chat about people we see.

39

"Hey, Tilly!" Mia says, and sticks her elbow into me. "Check it out!"

A man has come up the stairs of the bus.

Does she mean check *him* out?

"He thinks he is *well* cool," Mia hisses.

The man has on a T-shirt, jeans and trainers.

He has sunglasses on the top of his shaved head.

His clothes look like they cost a lot of money.

I bet he *does* think he's cool.

"His bald head is like a big potato!" Mia blurts out.

Uh-oh.

She said that a bit too loud. And it didn't help that I burst into giggles.

The man frowns at us before he sits down.

"Well, it's true!" says Mia, with a grin.

"Shhhh!" I whisper, but I still have the giggles.

Other people on the bus are giving us the evil eye too, but Mia just gives them her best sweet smile.

What *is* she like?

Well, she's not like any other friend I've ever had.

Zoe, Grace and Helena were the friends I had before. They were nice, but not crazy, like Mia is.

But they're not my friends any more. Not since I got a place at Beech Cliff school.

When I told them I was going to Beech Cliff, they said, "Hmm, that's posh, isn't it?"

What they meant was "You think you're too good for us now, don't you?"

But it wasn't *my* fault I had to go there.

Hey, my parents are snobs, OK? They were happy for me to go to the local primary school at the end of our road.

But when it came to secondary school, they made me sit an exam to get into Beech Cliff.

I was sorry I passed that exam. Everyone else in my class went on to the school ten minutes' stroll away. But because I passed, I have to take two long bus journeys every day, all by myself.

Well, I was all by myself for the first two days, till I got to know Mia. I didn't spot her at first, among all the new faces.

Then I saw her in Mrs West's class, pulling a face behind Mrs West's back. I burst into giggles, and had to cover up the noise with a pretend sneeze.

I've been giggling ever since.

"Thanks!" I say now to Mia.

"What for?" she asks. "Getting you into trouble with the man who looks like a potato?"

I give her a joke slap on the arm.

"For making my first week at Beech Cliff so much fun, you idiot!" I tell her.

Me and Mia, we're BFFA*...

* BFFA = Best Friends Forever – Already!

Chapter 2
New Girl, New Friend?

It's nearly 9 am, and me and Mia are sitting on a bench in the playground.

We got here ten minutes earlier than we planned.

Which gave Mia ten extra minutes to make comments about other girls' bad haircuts and ugly shoes, while I giggled.

Then Mia gets up. "Back in a second," she says, and goes off to the toilet block. "Don't go into class without me!"

"OK," I shrug.

It's still a minute or two till the 9 am bell, and I'm happy hanging out here in the sunshine.

Until someone interrupts.

"Hi, can you tell me where the office is, please?"

I turn and see a girl I don't know. Not that it's a big surprise I don't know her – I've only been at Beech Cliff a week and a half. Apart from Mia and a few others in my form class, just about everyone's a stranger still.

"Sure," I say. "It's round the corner, at the North Door."

I may as well have said, "It's at the North Pole." The girl hasn't a clue where I mean.

"Sorry – I just started today," she says. "Can you maybe show me?"

I gaze over at the toilet block. I look at my watch. I bite my lip.

Then I make up my mind that Mia will be fine. I'll catch up with her in class. I have to help this person – I know how hard it is to be new at school.

As we wander between chatting groups of students, I get a good look at the new girl.

She has green eyes and light brown skin, and is smiley and pretty.

Her dark, curly hair is pulled into two short, stubby plaits. It's kind of cute.

"How come you're so late starting term?" I ask.

"We went to visit my granny in Barbados, and there was a hurricane," she tells me. "Our flight home got delayed for days, 'cause of the storm."

"Wow," I say.

I'm thinking 'wow – a hurricane' AND 'wow – this girl has a granny in Barbados!'

My granny lives about a mile away from our house, and last time I went to see her it was a bit rainy.

Not exactly Barbados!

"Is this it?" the girl asks, as we reach the North Door. She seems nervous.

"Yes," I say. I walk up the steps hold the door open for her.

The lady in the office slides the glass window open and barks "Yes?" at us.

"Um, I'm supposed to be starting in Year 7 today," says the girl.

"Right." The woman nods as she turns to her computer. "Name?"

"Amber Sweet," the girl tells her.

Amber Sweet! Her name is as cute as her stubby plaits.

"Hold on ... got to get your details up," the office lady says. She sounds bored.

As we wait, Amber nibbles at her nail and turns to me.

"Is it – is it OK here?" she whispers. She sounds nervous again. "It's just that I'm the only one from my primary school who got in here, and I feel kind of shy ..."

Right away I feel sorry for her. I know how she feels. I remember how much I needed a friend on my first day at Beech Cliff.

"Don't worry," I say. "We'll show you round, me and – "

Before I can say Mia's name, I hear my own name being shouted.

"Tilly? Why didn't you wait? Oh ..."

I turn around and see Mia staring.

Staring hard at Amber Sweet.

Is there something I should know ...?

Chapter 3
Two Sorts of Smiles

All around us, plates clatter and girls chatter.

The long tables in the dining hall are almost full, but me and Mia have grabbed one of the small tables by the window for ourselves.

"Feeling better?" I ask Mia.

She is wolfing down her tuna pasta.

Three hours ago she'd freaked me out – she had been staring at Amber the new girl like she hated her.

But I'd got it all wrong. Mia had been feeling sick. She'd thought she was about to throw up all over the 'Welcome To Beech Cliff' doormat.

I'd had to leave Amber at the office and take Mia to the medical room as fast as I could, before things got messy.

A glass of ice water and a cool cloth on her head had soon sorted her out.

"Mmm! I'm feeling much better," Mia grins, between bites.

She looks so pretty, even with tomato sauce on her chin. It's her wide catty eyes and her long, sandy hair. If there were boys at our school I bet they'd all fancy her.

"Hi ... could I maybe sit here with you?"

I glance up to see Amber Sweet standing by the table. She smiles down at us hopefully.

"Of course!" I say, and take my bag off the spare chair.

"Thanks!" beams Amber.

This close, her eyes look as green as new leaves. I notice for the first time that she has dimples when she smiles, and she seems to smile a lot.

She's smiling at Mia now.

"Oh, you guys didn't meet properly before, did you?" I say. "Mia – this is Amber. Amber, this is Mia!"

Amber's smile is like sunshine. Mia's looks as real as one painted on a plastic doll. Maybe she's sick again?

"Which class did they put you in?" I ask Amber.

"7C," she says. "The other girls seem OK, but they're all friends already."

"You'll get to know everyone soon," I say, to make her feel better. "So, anyway, what's Barbados like?"

I'm dying to know all about it. I'd love to go to the West Indies one day. My family have only been as far as France on holiday.

"Great!" says Amber. "Here, look ..." She pulls out her phone and shows us photos of beautiful beaches and happy people.

"Is that your mum?" I ask, as she lets me see a photo of a very pretty woman.

"Yes," Amber says.

"You look just like her!" I tell her. But then she bursts into giggles.

"It's funny you think that," she says. "I'm actually adopted!"

"Are you?" I say in surprise. I've never met anyone who's adopted before.

"Uh-huh," Amber nods.

"What about your *real* parents?" Mia asks all of a sudden.

"Mum and Dad *are* my real parents" Amber says. "I've been with them since I was a baby. I don't remember my birth parents."

"So why didn't you stay with your birth parents?" Mia asks.

Amber's sunshine smile has started to fade.

I don't think Mia means to be rude, but I think that question is a bit too personal. I try to change the subject.

"Hey – that looks fun!" I say, and point to a photo of Amber waving from a rollercoaster. "Is that a theme park in Barbados?"

Amber smiles at me, like she's glad to talk about something else.

"No – that's at Alton Towers, here in Britain. My uncle works there. We get free passes all the time!"

"Wow!" I say.

I seem to say 'wow' a lot when it comes to Amber Sweet.

But Mia says nothing at all.

She is very quiet.

Her arms are folded across her chest.

My BFFA is thinking something and I'm pretty sure it's *not* 'wow'...

Chapter 4
Fakes and Fairy Stories

3.36pm.

The number 39 bus.

Mia has her feet pressed up against the back of the seat in front.

She is tapping them in time to the music on her iPod.

The woman in that seat looks around, annoyed.

Mia has her earphones in and is staring out of the bus window, so I mouth "sorry" at the lady instead.

I poke Mia. I don't know why she has her iPod on instead of chatting with me, like normal.

Come to think about it, she's been a bit weird with me all afternoon. She didn't even speak to me in class.

"What's up?" I ask, when Mia takes the earphones out.

"You!" she snaps. "You are so dumb to fall for her lies, Tilly!"

Huh?

What does Mia mean?

Who is she talking about?

Mia sees me frown and rolls her eyes.

"Amber Sweet!" she says. "She is just *such* a fake! And you listened to all her stupid fairy stories and believed every single one!"

"What – you think she was *lying*?" I ask, stunned.

"Of *course* she was!" Mia laughs. "All that stuff she told us at lunchtime ... she was just showing off. She made it all up to impress you. And it worked!"

"But how do you *know* she was lying?" I ask. I feel totally confused.

"Because there was a girl at my primary school that was just like her," Mia says. "She was always boasting about 'amazing' things that had happened to her. Then we found out it was a load of big fat lies."

I blink as I listen to Mia's words.

OK, so Amber had told us tons about herself at lunchtime.

It wasn't just the stuff about being adopted or having an uncle who worked at Alton Towers.

She also said that she'd won heaps of ice-skating cups.

And that her grandad was once mayor of his town.

And that she'd been in a TV ad for kids' sunscreen when she was little.

It all sounded so ... interesting.

But *was* she just saying it to impress us?

"Are you *sure*?" I ask Mia.

"100 per cent," Mia says. "And here's how I know ... you were *right* about the photo."

"Which one?" I ask. Pictures of golden beaches spin round my muddled head.

"The one with Amber's mum," Mia says. "She does look very like her, so Amber *can't* be adopted!" Mia sounds pleased with herself. "*And* she didn't want to talk about her birth parents!" she goes on. "See?"

I got it now, sort of.

Amber had made it all up.

You know, it's lucky Mia is *way* smarter than me.

What would I do without my BFFA …?

Chapter 5
Avoiding Amber

If Amber had told us those stories to make herself popular, she failed.

"She's over there. Don't even look at her," Mia says the next day.

Amber is sitting on the school steps. Her face lights up at the sight of me and Mia as we come in the gate.

She smiles her dimply smile and waves. But Mia links her arm in mine and steers us in the other direction.

Out of the corner of my eye, I see Amber's smile fade.

It makes me feel bad, but then I remember it's her own fault.

If she hadn't tried so hard ... if she hadn't told us fairy stories that were just fibs ... Maybe we could have been friends, me and Mia and Amber.

Well, that was never going to happen now.

Thank goodness Mia sussed Amber out so fast, before it got hard to shake her off.

"Even her hair is stupid," Mia mutters as we walk away. "Those silly plaits. How old is she – five?"

I giggle, just like I always do.

'Cause Mia is my best friend.

And Mia is very funny.

But something is different ... and I can't work out what it is.

All I know is that I feel weird.

And I haven't been able to shake off the feeling all day.

Not at morning break, when Amber stared over at us. (I pretended to look at something on my phone.)

Not at lunch, when she came over and asked if she could sit with us again. ("Sorry, we're keeping this seat for someone," Mia lied.)

Not even now, when I nip to the loo between afternoon lessons ...

"Tilly?"

'Oh, no,' I think, as I look in the mirror and see Amber behind me.

She's just come out of one of the loos.

I don't say anything in reply. The truth is, I don't know *what* to say, 'cause Mia's not here to help me.

"Have I done something to upset you?" Amber asks.

Funny she's saying that, since *she's* the one who looks upset.

What am I supposed to tell her?

That she pretends she's all sweetness and light like her name, but she's more like sweetness and *lies*?

Instead, I do the only thing I can think of.

I turn and run away from her.

Chapter 6
Good Deeds and Bad Vibes

The bus is taking a long time to move off from the stop.

Apart from the crush of girls from school, a mum is trying to squeeze on with her buggy.

Mia is staring out of the top deck window. "Check out that baby," she says.

I stand up a little and peer down.

The mum is struggling – the buggy is heavy 'cause there are shopping bags on the handles.

"What about the baby?" I ask.

"It's like a little gremlin, isn't it?" Mia laughs.

I look harder.

The little kid looks like most babies do – round, wriggly and cute.

"Doesn't it?" ask Mia, again.

I turn and see that she looks puzzled. She expects me to giggle, but my face is blank.

"I dunno – it looks kind of sweet," I say.

"Are you alright?" Mia frowns. "You've been a bit quiet today."

Again, I don't answer her straight away.

This time it's because now I'm watching someone do a good deed.

Amber Sweet has just rushed along the pavement and grabbed the front of the buggy. With a quick lift, she's helped the mum get her kid and shopping onto the bus.

I hear the mum's voice drift up from the bottom deck. "Thank you!" she says. "Thank you so much!"

"Oh, no ... SHE'S not getting on, is she?" Mia mutters.

She's staring down at the top of Amber's head. If Mia's eyes were lasers, Amber would be in *big* trouble.

"No – she's walking away," I say, and sit back down.

"Good!" Mia says. "Hey, look what Sarah from 7B is wearing!"

But I don't care what Sarah from 7B wearing.

I'm too busy watching Amber.

She's trailing after a big crowd of girls, all going home. The other girls all chat and smile. Amber's on her own and frowning.

As the packed bus moves off, I have to turn my head to see her.

Mia notices – she stops staring at Sarah whatsit and swivels her face round to see what *I'm* seeing.

"Hey, don't waste your time thinking about Amber!" she tells me.

"I know," I mumble. "But I just feel a bit sorry for her ..."

"Are you crazy, Tilly?" Mia asks. "If she's anything like the girl I knew in primary, she'll move on."

"To another school?" I say. I'm in a panic now. Will Amber leave Beech Cliff just 'cause of me and Mia?

Even if Amber IS a liar, I don't like to think I've helped drive her away ...

"No, Dumbo!" Mia says, and rolls her eyes at me. "I mean she'll move onto some other mug like you, who'll believe her show-off stories."

Mia's right.

Of course she is.

I just wish I didn't feel so ... so what, exactly?

A jumble of bad, sad, mean and miserable, *that's* what.

Chapter 7
Can it Be *My* Mia?

Around about 3.50pm every day, we arrive at Mia's bus stop and I wave her off.

But not today.

As if today wasn't bad enough already, now I have to go to the dentist.

So at 3.45, it's *me* getting off first, and Mia doing the waving.

"Hey, Tilly – don't scream too loud when the needle goes in. Aaaarghhhhh!" she yells, as I ring the bell for the bus to stop, and stomp down the stairs.

I smile, even though I don't feel like it.

I smile some more as I see her pull a face at me out of the back window, before the bus turns the corner.

And then I can relax and let my face do what it wants.

Which is sag into a puzzled frown ...

"Tilly?"

I'm expecting to meet Mum in a few minutes, here at the bus stop. But that's not her voice.

I look up and see Charlotte thingummy. I can't remember her last name. She wasn't at my primary school but we did swimming lessons together, back in Year 5.

"Hi, Charlotte!" I reply.

She was nice, I think now. We used to chat so much the swimming teacher would tell us off.

I notice Charlotte's wearing a uniform for the secondary school round the corner from my dentist.

"So you're at Beech Cliff, Tilly?" Charlotte asks, as *she* takes in *my* uniform. "How's that going?"

"Not bad," I shrug. "Don't like the long bus journey much. But it's OK – I've made friends with a girl called Mia, and she comes part of the way with me."

"Mia? Mia who?" Charlotte asks.

"Thomson," I tell her. "Mia Thomson."

From the look on Charlotte's face, she knows that name. And she knows *my* Mia, I guess.

But Charlotte's not smiling like people always do when they know someone in common.

"She was at my primary school," Charlotte says. "But Tilly, you *do* realise what she's like, don't you?"

"I ... well, yes ..." I stutter. "She's my best friend and she's really funny and ..." My brain trips me up and I stop. I can't think straight.

Charlotte doesn't think much of Mia, I can tell.

"Listen," she says. "I don't mean to be horrible, Tilly, but Mia Thomson is *not* a nice person."

Now my brain feels like total mush – as scrambled as an egg.

"Maybe it's a different girl, with the same name?" I say hopefully.

"Does she have blondey-brown hair, down to about here?" Charlotte's hand hovers down below her neck, right about where Mia's hair comes.

"Well, yeah," I shrug. "But loads of girls have hair like that, don't they?"

"Well, yes," says Charlotte, with a shrug of her own. "But is she really pretty, with eyes like a Siamese cat?"

I gulp.

It *is* my Mia she's talking about.

And of course I know Mia went to Victoria Park School, where Charlotte went too. Me and

Mia talked about it on the first day we became friends. We chatted about our old schools and our *old* friends.

Our old friends who didn't want to know us any more, 'cause our parents had sent us to Beech Cliff.

Hey, maybe that's what's wrong with Charlotte! Like my old buddies Zoe, Grace and Helena, she could be weird about Mia going to the 'posh' school.

Is Charlotte being unkind about Mia 'cause she's jealous?

"Mia's OK!" I try to tell her. "You just mustn't know her. She's a good laugh!"

"Oh, yes, Mia's a good laugh, alright," says Charlotte. She's gone all sarky. "She's good at taking the mickey out of people. She doesn't ever stop, not even if she upsets them."

"No! She's not like that! She wouldn't ..." My sentence drifts off. Charlotte is right. On the bus home from school, Mia's *always* saying stuff that's funny to us, but not to the person she's talking about.

Now I come to think about it, she's like that to *me* too!

Before I can take that in, Charlotte starts again. "At Victoria Park, she was famous for ..."

Charlotte tells me story after story about Mia, and only stops when, at last, Mum arrives to meet me.

"Oh, Tilly, honey!" says Mum, as Charlotte waves and walks off. "Look at your face! I'm sure the dentist won't be that bad!"

But Mum has got it all wrong.

It's not the dentist I'm scared of.

It's my own lousy taste in so-called BFFAs ...

WEST HILL
CITY
MAP

Chapter 8
How to Be Brave

"Cheer up! What's wrong with you this morning?" Mia demands.

She's standing over me.

I'm perched on the edge of a low wall round a flowerbed.

It's 8.55 am, and I've been waiting in the playground for ages.

Waiting to talk to Mia.

Waiting to get it over with.

"Did the dentist say you've got to get all your teeth out?" Mia asks. "Yeah, I can just imagine you all ugly like this!"

Mia covers her own teeth with her lips and makes a goofy, gummy face. "Oh, come on, Tilly! I'm just joking!" she says, when she sees I'm not smiling.

The thing is, I don't feel like smiling at anything Mia says.

I don't like her jokes any more.

And I don't like being called ugly.

Or 'Dumbo'.

Or stupid.

Or a mug.

Or anything *else* she's said to my face over the last week or so.

'Cause best friends don't say things like that to each other.

Mia frowns. "What's with you this morning?"

I take a deep breath and wonder how to be brave.

I've never had to be brave before.

That's because I've never had to stand up to someone as mean as Mia.

For a second, I stop. The words sit in my mouth, scared to come out.

Then, over by the gate, I see Amber Sweet walk in. She looks lonely and blue.

And then I know I can be as brave as I need to be.

"I heard about Becci Brown," I tell Mia. My voice sounds a little wobbly, but at least the words came out.

"What did you say?" Mia's nostrils have flared. Her eyes have narrowed. Instead of looking pretty, now she looks as cruel as I know she is, deep down.

"You heard."

Just two words.

Two words that make Mia Thomson so mad at me – or ashamed of herself – that she storms off.

Over near the gate, Amber Sweet stops. She's just seen Mia swoop away from me, with her face full of fury.

"Are you OK?" Amber mouths at me. She's too far away for me to hear her.

"Yes," I mouth back.

But my lips – like the rest of my body – are shaking ...

Chapter 9
Unhappy Endings

I'm still shaking as I wait outside my first class of the day.

My heart thumps madly.

I have to go in and face Mia – sit *next* to Mia.

I'm not sure I can do it after what just happened.

I think I've used up all my bravery for the day!

"Are you OK, Tilly?" someone asks.

I turn and see my teacher, Miss West. She pats my arm gently. She looks worried.

What can I say?

I wonder if I can tell her the truth about Mia ... all the stuff that Charlotte told me.

Where would I start?

So Mia likes to mess with people's friendships. (It's what she was famous for at her primary school.)

Mia hates it if her BFF ever gets matey with other people. (She wasn't sick that morning she met Amber – she was jealous and angry.)

Mia tells lies – lies that damage lives. (Poor Becci Brown ...)

The Becci Brown thing happened in Year 6. Mia made up her mind she wanted a girl called Jodie as her new best friend.

The trouble was, Jodie already *had* a BF – Becci Brown.

Mia had to get rid of Becci.

So she started to be a bit rude to her.

Then she started rumours about her.

One day, Jodie's watch went missing during PE.

Mia told everyone she'd seen Becci Brown near Jodie's locker.

Becci denied it, but no one knew what to think.

For weeks people stayed away from Becci, while Becci got sadder and sadder … and then left school.

And the watch? It turned up in the end – in Mia's locker.

Now it was *Mia's* turn to leave school … she got expelled, but too late to make a difference to poor Becci Brown.

"Tilly?" Miss West says. She is still waiting for an answer from me. "Has something happened?"

"It's me and Mia," I say. That's all.

The whole truth about Mia is *way* too much to tell Miss West, and the bell's about to jangle.

"Hmm. I'm not sure you two are good for each other," Miss West mutters. "There's always too much chatting and giggling going on. How about I move you to different tables?"

I think Mrs West expects me to say, “No way!”

Instead I surprise her – and myself – by giving her a hug to say thanks ...

Chapter 10

Me and My BFF – R&T!

"Hey, Tilly! Check it out!" Amber pokes me and points to a little kid down below.

The kid stares up at us. He's a boy, about three, and he has these huge round eyes.

"Doesn't he look like one of those cute toys everyone used to collect?" Amber says. "What were they called ... Oh, I know – Beanie Boos!"

She's right, I think, and I break into giggles.

Amber cracks me up.

She is *so* funny.

But the difference between her and Mia is that Amber's funny *without* being mean.

Oh, and in case you're wondering, the time is 3.35pm.

And me and Amber *aren't* on the top deck of the 39 bus.

It's Saturday and we're on the Sky Ride, a monorail way up above Alton Towers.

We got free passes, thanks to Amber's Uncle Stuart. He works in the marketing department at the theme park.

It turns out Amber's Uncle Stuart used to work for a firm that made sunscreen for kids. They wanted a cute little girl for their TV ad,

and he told them about Amber. That's why she ended up on telly when she was small.

Yes, *everything* about Amber is real and true.

She is very proud of her grandad, who was once mayor of the town he lives in. I've seen the photos of him in his robes and big gold chain of office, which proves it.

In fact, I've seen *lots* of stuff while I've been hanging out at Amber's house this last month.

She showed me the cabinet full of ice-skating cups in her bedroom.

And last week – when she knew she could really, truly trust me – she let me look at the album of photos of her when she was a baby, with her birth family.

I think she is very like her birth mother, but it's funny – she's even *more* like her real, adoptive mum.

"I think everyone has the same mannerisms as the family they grow up in," Amber explained, as she put the album away again, safe in a drawer.

She said she's not shown the album to a lot of people. That makes me feel pretty special.

"Shall we go on the Congo River Rapids after this, Tilly?" Amber asks now.

She points down to the splashy water ride raging below us.

"Yeah, OK!" I agree.

It looks a bit scary, but it's not so easy to scare me any more.

Not since I stood up to Mia Thomson.

Isn't it funny that she once talked about a girl at her primary school who lied to impress people and make friends?

All that time, she was talking about herself!

I guess she was pleased that no one from Victoria Park moved up to Beech Cliff.

I guess she thought she could start again, since no one would know about her past.

But Mia couldn't leave her mean streak behind.

She couldn't help the bad stuff creeping in, once she knew I was her best friend ...

"Are you OK, Tilly?" Amber asks.

"Yes!" I smile.

And I really am OK.

I've been better than OK ever since Mia switched to a different form class. I never see her any more. I heard she's told the girls in 7D that she was being 'bullied' in our class.

Ha!

Of course, it's just another one of her stupid lies, and I hope no one believes her.

But why am I wasting time thinking about my BFFN (Best Friend Forever – Never!)?

I'm up on the Sky Ride – on top of the world – with Amber Sweet, my Best Friend Forever, Real and True!

Our books are tested
for children and young people by
children and young people.

Thanks to everyone who consulted on
a manuscript for their time and effort in
helping us to make our books better
for our readers.